SUNFALL
MANOR

PETER GIGLIO

Sunfall Manor
Copyright © 2012 by Peter Giglio

This edition of Sunfall Manor
Copyright © 2012 by Nightscape Press, LLP

Cover illustration and design by William Cook
Cover lettering by Peter Giglio
Interior layout and design by Robert S. Wilson
Interior illustration by William Cook

Edited by Robert S. Wilson

First Edition

ISBN: 1-938644-05-0
ISBN-13: 978-1-938644-05-4

Nightscape Press, LLP
http://www.nightscapepress.com

Advance Praise for *Sunfall Manor*

"*Sunfall Manor* is a gem of a story that reminds me of Sherwood Anderson's *Winesburg, Ohio*...vignettes of lives lived and lost with touches of sadness, regret, and vengeance. A tale sure to send more than a few shivers up your spine...and your soul."

Rick Hautala, author of *Indian Summer* and *Little Brothers*

"Any horror fan who's properly awake has been following the crazily productive visionary exactitude of Peter Giglio. He slings plainsong toughness pressurized by pop-eyed mania. *Sunfall Manor*'s not his debut, though it's his debut masterpiece: A cold-trance-inducing, five-click merry-go-round about a rundown dwelling in the flatlands that feels more like a schizoid colony in outer space. This thing should be a major film, though we'll have to wake up Kubrick to do it right. A work of art that you'll be judged for missing."

Eric Shapiro, author of *The Devoted* and *It's Only Temporary*

"A lesser thinker might have been content with a haunted house story. A lesser storyteller might have been content with a tale of discovery, or perhaps of ghostly revenge. But Peter Giglio has more up his sleeve than ghosts and creepy old houses. He's even got more than mere philosophy."

Bram Stoker Award-winning author **Joe McKinney**, from his introduction

"Let Peter Giglio's odd protagonist, Edgar, take you on a surreal tour of the mysterious *Sunfall Manor* with its intriguing but flawed residents. Giglio's prose is highly accessible and very engaging, his story line equally compelling. This is Giglio playing at the top of his game, shooting and making all 3s. Highly recommended."

Gene O'Neill, author of *The Burden of Indigo* and *Operation Rhinoceros Hornbill*

"Peter Giglio's *Sunfall Manor* is a gripping ghost story that will possess your mind like a crazed poltergeist. Psychological horror at its best."

Jeremy C. Shipp, Bram Stoker nominated author of *Vacation* and *Cursed*

"A powerful, moving, intimate look into private lives we would rather deny, but all have lived, in one way or another. Giglio's writing is clear, insightful, and fueled with a potent and intoxicating intimacy. To read *Sunfall Manor* is to take a poetic journey through truths, falsehoods, hopes, dreams and failures that comprise the human condition. And it's truly haunting."

Trent Zelazny, author of *Butterfly Potion*

"Haunting and unforgettable, *Sunfall Manor* is Mr. Giglio's finest work to date. Period! This vivid and revealing shocker begs to be made into a movie and further cements him as the rising star that he is."

David Bernstein, author of *Amongst the Dead* and *Tears of No Return*

"*Sunfall Manor* is as much a character study of lost and damaged souls as it is a horror story. Giglio is an excellent writer who is not afraid to show the bleak human condition at its ugliest. Well done!"

Tracy L. Carbone, co-chair of New England Horror Writers, author of *The Soul Collector*, and Bram Stoker nominated editor of *Epitaphs*.

"In Sunfall Manor, Peter Giglio reinvents the ghost story. Life and afterlife are examined through the eyes of a dead man, and it's like looking through a dust-filled kaleidoscope. Raw human emotion and exploration of the human condition in the rural midwest are Giglio's specialty. This story will stay with you long after you close the book. Very highly recommended."

S. S. Michaels, author of Revival House and Idols & Cons

Existence, Essence and the Existentialism of Ghosts
By Joe McKinney

John D. MacDonald, one of the literary gods I worship, once wrote: "You send books out into the world and it is very hard to shuck them out of the spirit. They are tangled children, trying to make their way in the world in spite of the handicaps you have imposed upon them."

Being both a father and a writer, I can promise you that truer words were never spoken.

Here's the issue: Books are living things. They possess a life of their own, one the writer can't control, no matter how adept he or she may be at marketing and salesmanship and all the other things that come with the business side of writing. You send the book out into the world, and like a child leaving home, it takes the raw stuff it's made of and becomes something the writer—or, if you will, the parent—never intended.

You see, like it or not, once you publish a book, it no longer belongs to you. You own the rights, but that's different. What you don't own, and what ultimately defines a book, is the experience the reader has while curled up with your book in the small hours of the night, or while sipping their morning coffee, or while daydreaming about the story when they should be running a board meeting or cleaning windows or whatever the hell people do all day. You can never own that moment, because that's private. In fact, I'd say the interaction between reader and text is about as close to intimacy as people can achieve outside of sex.

And, of course, being human, we can't help but share such an intensely intimate moment with anyone who will listen.

This is how books join the larger community of readers, how they take on a global meaning beyond the intimate experience of reader and text.

Books, in other words, are like people making their way in the world, building a reputation. Some do it well, some languish in obscurity, and some stumble blindly from point to point, constantly struggling for identity and meaning.

Sound like anyone you know?

I'm willing to guess more than one.

But just on the offhand chance that you've never met someone like that, someone stumbling blindly through an absurd universe, looking for answers that will perhaps never materialize, Peter Giglio is about to introduce you to one in the character of Edgar.

Edgar, you see, is a ghost: a ghost who is whiling away eternity in an existentialist nightmare; a ghost who is trapped in an endless cycle of addiction, self-loathing, lust, narcissism and benevolent buffoonery. All of these things make up the facticity of Edgar's existence. Or at least the limitations of Edgar's facticity, for they cannot, and do not, ultimately, define him in his totality.

Why not?

Well, you see, Edgar has made a set of values for himself. A code, if you will. Edgar lives by this code. He witnesses the parade of human depravity all around him, and for a long time, has stayed above it, apart from it, all the while wondering what possible purpose he is meant to serve. He's trying to understand who he is — or, rather, was — and yes, he's fully capable of the empathy necessary to evaluate and understand the Others with whom he shares his hellish existence, but unlike the Others, Edgar is capable of so much more.

For you see, in true Existentialist fashion, Edgar is a trailblazer. He is in the process of remaking himself, of self-making, if you will, because he has no one else to help him on that voyage. And he's capable of making that voyage because, to him, there is a future, and he is a part of it. He sees beyond the limitations of his ghostly existence. He's not questioning the external possibilities of a spiritual otherworld, he's questioning his own ability to become something other than what he currently is. You see, Edgar's voyage is through an interior landscape. There is no light to go in to. There is only a sense that one is responsible for one's actions, one's values.

Edgar makes mistakes. He makes ghastly mistakes.

People die because of his mistakes.

And yet, through it all, Edgar searches for a meaning, for a purpose. Spiritual redemption is not part of the equation that needs balancing. What does need balancing is Edgar's sense of justice. He has an internal value system that has been offended by events beyond his control, and to a degree which offends on the most atavistic level imaginable, and when Edgar finally finds the traction he needs to pursue that offense, his story changes from one of Existential self-examination to abject horror.

The subtlety of that shift is perhaps the most delightful display of Peter Giglio's genius in *Sunfall Manor*. A lesser thinker might have been content with a haunted house story. A lesser story teller might have been content with a tale of discovery, or perhaps one of ghostly revenge.

But Peter Giglio has more up his sleeve than ghosts and creepy old houses.

He's even got more than mere philosophy.

What he's got, and what I loved about his tale, and what I suspect you'll love about his tale, is his sense of story.

In these pages, you see, story is king.

If you don't have story, you don't have anything worth reading.

And Peter Giglio's *Sunfall Manor* is worth reading.

In fact, I'm sorry you spent so much time on these pages, because while you were reading about my thoughts on Existentialism, and how Edgar is a stand-in, an Everyman, for the interior journey through the absurd that every thinking person (and every published book) must make on their own, you could have spent that time reading Peter Giglio's tale.

I envy those of you about to encounter this story for the first time, because you've got a lot of thinking ahead of you.

You've got worlds to discover.

Joe McKinney
San Antonio, Texas
June 27, 2012

To Scott Bradley,
the best writing partner and friend in the world.

– I –

Edgar

When he first arrived at Sunfall Manor, a lopsided farmhouse divided into five apartments, he didn't know he was a ghost. His entire identity was a mystery to him, yet he wasn't devoid of knowledge. And ghosts, as far as he was concerned, couldn't move things easily in the world of the living. Although he didn't know the origin of that notion— or the origin of anything he knew or thought he knew—he clung to it, unwilling to diagnose his malady if the symptoms weren't just right. He touched a drapery, and it fluttered. Not a ghost, simple as that.

He searched his mind for a name. All things deserve a name, he told himself; even diseases have names. But he came up blank… until, while trying unsuccessfully to piss, desperate to uncover traits of the human condition within himself, he was struck by a name that carried understated dignity: Edgar. Everything else askew, that name rang right. Not the most flattering title, of course, but monikers like Thor and Apollo and Hercules were way too godly for someone so completely lost. Edgar was an admirable name, respectable, one, he sensed, he could grow into.

The first thing he really grabbed, not just moved, was a fat glass of gin. Tried to drink it, too, certain he needed such tonics—he needed something—but the liquid fell though his throat and splashed onto the floor. This gave Art Stillwater, the jigger's owner, one hell of a scare, but his terror didn't last. A few moments of wide eyes and blanched flesh—Art stammering like a child who'd been caught doing wrong, something for which he couldn't construct a proper excuse—came to a halt when Art blinked several times, shook his head, and poured a fresh drink.

"The mind's a monkey," Art said, as if that explained anything. Then he slammed the drink down in one gulp, poured another.

Art, Edgar would come to learn, was like that. Powerful moments that should have meant something, should have at least brought a degree of dawning awareness, washed away quickly in the haze of his one true obsession; that and copious booze.

Edgar talked *at* Art for hours, even said he was sorry, though he really wasn't. But Art paid Edgar less mind than the spilled alcohol on the cracked linoleum, a mess that evaporated over time with no bodily intervention, human or ethereal.

A few nights later—Art sitting at his desk with his head in his hands—Edgar found himself staring at the living room's south wall, inspecting the piss-poor paint job. He traced the outline of burn marks with a gentle touch. Gray slashes spread toward the ceiling, terminating in an upside-down V. When his finger, applying mild pressure to the highest point of the poorly disguised damage, painlessly seeped through the plaster, he knew more. Walking through the wall, he knew what he was. No denying his situation now. Still, the mystery of *who* he was remained unsolved. He didn't know whether to be comforted or terrified by that.

He spent several nights trying to breach the walls that bordered the outside world, but those barriers, clearly the fortifications of his cell, proved impassable. So he just trudged through five different worlds, each of them painful and pitiful and terrifying.

Check your clocks. The time is now...

And Edgar still spends his nights roaming, hoping to learn. But, like trying to solve a puzzle with pieces from different boxes, nothing fits.

Instead he answers easier questions, like the odd title of his bleak home. "Sunfall" is easy—the town's name, a rural burg with a population of less than five hundred. He knows this from the many newspapers he reads. But the "Manor" part is just a bunch of pretentious bullshit, near as he can tell, an effort to give this shit-hole a modicum of dignity.

Like Edgar, he thinks, and laughs at himself mirthlessly.

There is little peace here. Daylight hours, when

this tomb's misbegotten denizens sleep, would provide Edgar ample opportunity to make sense of his internment. Such is not his lot in death, for the day grants him no sentience.

Where he goes when dawn peeks over the flat Nebraska horizon, he doesn't know. He doesn't care. That is a time when *forgetting* becomes complete, no longer a waking nightmare, nothing replacing something. He wishes he could go there forever.

Although he doesn't know his real name, his family—if he had one—or what he did in life, he remembers wars, books, TV shows and movies. He remembers the scandals and silly algebraic equations. He remembers what a woman tastes like. These things, however, grant nothing. He's not sure they ever did anyone any good.

All that he really owns now are the dreary nights at Sunfall Manor.

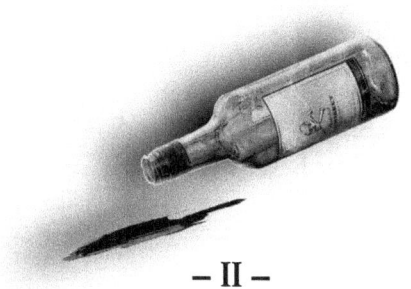

– II –

Art

A rt's in rare form tonight, sitting in front of the television and eating pizza. And he's smiling. He smiles less frequently than he eats, which is almost never.

This place is where Edgar always starts, in the unit with clear burn marks beneath the paint. He suspects that has something to do with why his rounds commence here. Not that suspicion grants insight. If that were the case, the residents of Sunfall Manor would be bona fide sages, and Art would be their leader.

Art breaks into wild laughter. And Edgar regards this curiously. He's never heard Art laugh. Then Art takes a big bite, laughs again with his mouth full. Edgar wants him to stop, Art's high-pitched braying is putting him on edge. Besides, the shit that's happening on the tube isn't even worthy of a chortle, just some lame-brain sitcom about a couple of girls who are trying to make a bunch of cash, reasons unclear.

"My cold streak's over," Art says. And Edgar, immediately knowing what he's talking about, walks over to Art's computer, where a file titled *Autumn's Child* is still open. Bet the asshole didn't even save his work, thinks Edgar. Then he considers deleting the file.

"That's why I'm probably here," Edgar says, not that it does him any good to speak aloud, "to torment these poor fuckers."

He reads what's on the screen. The only two words that really fit together are "Chapter" and "One." The rest is pure crap, and Edgar knows that deleting the file would be an act of mercy. At least Art would *think* he'd produced something great. When Art reads this, Edgar muses, he's going to plunge deeper into the abyss. But Edgar can't bring himself to grant Art mercy anymore than he can intentionally inflict harm. Just like the dumb girls on Art's new favorite show, his reasons are unclear. Damning his code, now *he* wants to laugh.

Art picks up the phone and punches buttons. "Hey, Lisa," he says.

"Why do you do this to yourself?" Edgar asks. "Isn't it bad enough that her photographs are all over the place?"

"No, no," Art says, though not to Edgar, "this is big. I-I got some writing done today."

Art goes quiet, and a voice like a catfight screeches from the receiver. He holds the phone away from his ear, cringes, and takes a swig of beer.

"Of course it's good," Art says. "It's the beginning of *Autumn's Child*, the book I always said I'd write for you. This one's more yours than mine. I cracked the opening, now I'm unstoppable."

Her feral cadence returns, and Edgar thinks about heading over to the Simmons place, the second haunt on his nightly rounds. *No*, he warns himself. *Too early.*

"Yeah, I'll read you what I've got so far," Art says. And Edgar has to stay for *this*. He takes no pleasure in Art's pain, nor does he relish any of the tiny emotional earthquakes at Sunfall Manor. But this is all he has, and it feels wrong to miss the money shots. He likens it to the reality TV these people watch, or the inability to look away from an accident. You don't really want to see what's coming next, you just have to.

Art sits down at his desk. "C'mon," he says, "it'll only take a minute." He holds the phone away from his ear as she berates him again, then says, "Okay, okay, here it is." He starts reading about a girl who grew up poor in New Orleans.

Edgar leans over Art's shoulder and puts his ear close to the phone. Not a word of the prose is genuine or well-written, and Art's face darkens by swift degrees as he reads. About fifty words into the mess he's cobbled together, Art's voice trails off.

"Five years," Lisa says. "Five years of my life wasted with you, and you don't know the first thing about me, or what I went through as a child. Why do you even try?"

"I'm sorry," Art mutters.

"Do you think you're gonna get me back if you

capture me on the page? Is that what you think?"

"No, I…"

A click, then the line goes dead.

"Lisa?" he pleads. But she's gone. Has clearly been gone for a long time. And he's left only with a flat-line dial tone and his many photographs. Smiles, frowns, looks of surprise: reminders of what will never again be, probably never really was.

Art deletes the file, shuts down the computer, and skulks back to the couch. Edgar sits next to him and watches tears trail down Art's twitchy face. Art takes another long pull from his beer bottle, turns the TV off, and picks up the pizza box, most of its contents still unconsumed. He walks to the front door, opens it, tosses his dinner into the yard, and shouts, "Come and get it, Sheppy."

He calls all the neighborhood dogs Sheppy. Sometimes even sits on the porch and talks to them like they're real people. "I'd take you in, Sheppy," Edgar once heard Art tell one of the mutts, "but I got it worse than you. Wouldn't be fair. Not fair at all. Besides, my money'll run out soon. Inheritance from working-class parents only goes so far in this world. And then you'd just be back on the streets. Don't wanna shine you on with false hope." The bedraggled hound had just stared up at him with sad, stupid eyes, clearly wanting food rather than excuses.

Art sits down at his desk and glares at the blank screen. Edgar wants to know what he's thinking and also doesn't. Then again, it doesn't take a mind-reader, which Edgar is not, to see that Art's wallowing in self-pity. Edgar wishes he could feel sympathy for him, that he could do something to help, but he can't. More accurately, he won't. Edgar's self-prescribed code is simple: *Don't get involved.*

Not that he's devoid of emotions or compassion. When one of the residents buys a newspaper, usually for the classifieds, or accidentally leaves the news on, Edgar pays attention. His heart bleeds for the victims in stories—nature-related disasters, child abductions, soldiers who won't be coming home. These are people he'd like to help, if given a chance.

So why have I been put here?

Art's the worst kind of victim. The self-inflicted sort. Edgar has read Art's published books, all two of them. They're the only volumes on his shelves, and Art never notices when Edgar takes them to the attic, the place he escapes once his rounds are completed. He's tried to jump rungs in the cycle, move straight to the attic, but it doesn't work. Access denied. Not only does he have to make these rounds, he has to spend sufficient time in each dwelling. He doesn't know how the clockwork of death works, but he's getting a good feel for it, and knows he is a low priority in the universe's scheme, if there is such a thing.

He's never had more than twenty minutes in the attic. When he's not reading Art's books up there, he reads old newspapers—the space is dense with them, all from the mid-to-late eighties. *Someone should really get rid of those old papers,* Edgar thinks. But no one, except for him, goes to the attic anymore. Not that Edgar's really anyone.

Art's books are all right in Edgar's estimation; pulp mystery novels, nothing more, but well-written and engaging. A far cry better than the stuff he's turned out since Edgar's arrival, which is next to nothing.

The old newspapers, copies of the local rag, are less fun; amateur musings about small town shit. But Edgar works through them anyway, hopeful—albeit doubtful—he'll eventually learn something about himself.

Now Art's uncapping a fifth of cheap bourbon. "Graduating from beer a little early tonight, aren't we, Art?" Edgar asks then shakes his head. Art guzzles from the bottle, staring at his menagerie of photographs, strewn haphazardly upon a goldenrod display that's long lost its luster.

"Lisa," Art says, "why do you hurt me?" Then he takes another long drink, all the irony of the moment clearly lost on him. A few minutes of silence grind by, the only noise coming from the ready-for-the-junkyard furnace that's struggling to warm these cold environs. Art snatches a portrait from the shelf and throws it to the floor. The frame shatters, then he pours some of the bourbon on the detritus and says, "I love you," in an emotionless monotone.

Art stumbles into the bathroom. The sound of the toilet seat going up. Pissing. Then a long silence. Edgar walks to the open bathroom door, watches his subject study himself in the mirror. Art plays with his curly hair, tilts his head, plays with his hair some more. His eyes go wide, then he squints, then they're wide again. He's breathing heavily.

"Why are you watching me?" Art says.

And Edgar is nakedly ashamed. Reflexively, he turns away from Art and says, "I'm sorry."

"Stop watching me," Art growls. "Quit judging

me."

Edgar casts his attention back on Art, who is now glaring and pointing at his reflection. His reflection, of course, is doing the same thing, and that seems to enrage him further.

The phone rings, and Art relaxes his expression. He gives himself a quick nod, then rushes, balance awkward, into the living room. Picks up the phone. "Hello…hey, Timmy-boy, thanks for calling me back," he says, slurring every S. "Nah, well, yeah, I'm okay. Just…you know…a lot of false starts—writer stuff. I'm sure you have similar…yeah…yeah…yeah…"

Intrigued, Edgar walks behind Art and puts his ear close to the phone.

"…just that Trish and I think you'd be better off here in California…" the voice on the other end says, Edgar continuing to chime in with "yeah" every few seconds, "…where you'll be close to family. We can get you back in therapy, and I talked to Julian, who says he can get you some work writing for Mexican TV. You have to understand how much we worry about you out there in—"

"I like it out here in the middle of nowhere," Art says. "You know how it was in LA, got to the point I couldn't go out in public anymore. I'm alone out here, no one watching me. Just how I like it."

If only he knew the truth.

"Are you able to leave the house in Nebraska?"

"Sure, I go to the grocery store. Not much else to do. No coffee shops or movie theatres. And no fucking traffic. Again, just the way *I* like it."

"Tell me this, what percentage of your purchases at the grocery store are liquor?"

"Hey, what kind of question—"

"I'm your brother, Arthur, and I love you very much. Thought about you yesterday when I visited Mom and Dad's grave. You should have been there with me, could have paid your respects and put some flowers—"

"No," Art says. "I can't be there. I thought we'd gone over this. Why don't you—"

"We can get you back into therapy, Arthur," the voice says again. "Are you seeing anyone professionally out there? Is there even anyone *to* see out there?"

"I don't need—"

"Stop it with the denial and try to look at this from my perspective—this is madness."

"Let's not talk about me anymore," Art says. "I…I really don't want to hear anymore disappointment from my *baby* brother."

"I'm sorry, Arthur, but I can tell you've been drinking. You promised you wouldn't drink if we let you—"

"No more about me, little man," Art shouts. "I called you 'cause I need help—real help! I'm almost out of money, and I was wondering if—"

"No more money, Arthur. If you want a place to live, you have one rent free. But it's not out there in the sticks, it's here with—"

Art hangs up the phone and throws it across the room. Beginning to breathe heavily again, like a child ready to throw a tantrum, he trudges back to the bathroom. Glares into the mirror for a few seconds, then punches his reflection.

Glass shatters. Blood runs down his wrist. He drops to his knees, clutching his injured fist, weeping like a newborn.

And Edgar's left asking the same question that he's asked more times than he cares to count. "Why am I here?" Then a flurry of thoughts: *Is it just to witness these things that would otherwise go unseen? If a tree falls in the forest, and no one's around, does it make a sound? Am I the answer to that old chestnut? Am I the universe's way to fill the void, to make moments that would otherwise go unremembered real?*

Pretty shitty job, if you ask me.

It's not like Art's going to remember any of this, regardless of physical scars. He called Lisa one night and repeated, "Fuck you, little bitch," over and over until she hung up. He called her the next night and, when confronted with his transgressions, swore the incident had never taken place. Edgar could tell that Art believed what he was saying. Every falsehood fell from his tongue with enough conviction to beat a polygraph.

She's just as bad as him, of course, answering the phone, prolonging his suffering. In a twisted way, Edgar's sure Art and Lisa deserved each other once upon a time.

But Edgar knows deep down that he's not here to make any of this real.

Exhibit A: Carolyn and Ralph Simmons. They never forget anything.

Edgar wonders what kind of wrong is cooking at the Simmons place tonight. Then he wonders about the time. He glances at Art's VCR. The clock flashes 12:00. No help there.

He shrugs and slips through the burn-scarred wall.

– III –

Carolyn

She's sitting in Ralph's chair, cross-stitching. This is where she always sits when he's out, a thing that, since the night Ralph swore he'd change his ways, happens less frequently than it used to. It was bound to start again. Ralph's word plus a nickel is worth five cents.

Ralph never returns reeking of booze. His sins are much greater, at least in Carolyn's mind. He comes home smelling of strange women. His eyes tell Edgar that Carolyn's suspicions are probably right.

Edgar looks over her shoulder. She's stitching a butterfly. Above the insect she's already embroidered *God is Good*. A copy of the King James lays on the end table beside her. In about thirty minutes, she'll put down her craftwork and pick up The Word. Her eyes will scan the pages, much like Edgar with his old newspapers, looking for something that isn't there. That used to make him feel a connection to her, though hardly a strong one. Not anymore. She, unlike Edgar, has the power to abandon her post. And she should.

She won't. And Edgar grows tired of studying her. He doesn't hate her, and that makes her a more frustrating subject than most. He paces around the apartment and tries not to think.

Sometimes he can enter a numb zone, a state where time seems to quicken—and he's not so certain it doesn't. Like most things, however, trying is the fastest route away from success. Besides, riding the numb zone usually cuts him off from attic time. And he senses that he must go there tonight, though he suspects it will, as always, lead to nothing.

Carolyn is crying now, and Edgar turns to face her. She's stabbing her hand with the stitching needle, little pools of blood welling in her palm. Looking away from her wounds, like a terrified child in a doctor's office, she stares at the Bible, a red leather-bound copy—the most expensive item in the entire apartment, Edgar surmises. Not that he's an expert on price tags.

Carolyn's got a photo on the wall of her and Bob Barker to prove she's taken a shot at such determinations. She watches the video tape sometimes. Her fifteen minutes of fame. Every answer, the price is wrong. No wonder she turns to Scripture. Dangerous for one so prone to misinterpretation. Same thing with her view of Ralph, only that's a far more perilous and poisonous vine.

So she *is* a prisoner. Her undying devotion to Ralph, Edgar can't fathom. She clings to him when he's here, caters to his every desire, talks sweetly though it's clear she's crumbling within. Perhaps that's what drives him away, hoping that when he returns she'll be gone, knowing that she's too good for him.

She is.

Carolyn's not a bad-looking woman by any measure, and she's young enough for a fresh start. A little plain maybe, but that's by choice, and par for the course in these prairie wilds. No children to tie her down, she's smart enough to take the pill behind Ralph's back. He just thinks she's infertile. A much more convincing liar than Ralph, she plays along with that verdict, demonstrating Oscar-worthy aplomb. A contradiction of her tragic condition, but a spark of hope nonetheless.

She may forgive his trespasses, but she never forgets. Forgetting is not Ralph's forte, either. Edgar can still hear the echoes of their last fight.

"Remember when you sent your mother our rent money so that she could take a trip?" Carolyn cries.

"She's my mother. She was sad, needed to get away."

"Maybe we should get away. Do you ever think about that? Unless…maybe you spent the money on someone else. One of your whores?"

"Remember when I took you to Austin? You complained about the heat the whole time, wouldn't even leave the hotel room. Why should I take you anywhere?"

"Didn't stop you from leaving the room."

"Had to get away from you, bitch."

"You could have tried harder."

"Like you try? Last time you put on makeup, Slick Willy was still in the White House."

This continues for hours, never going anywhere. Physical violence never rears its ugly head—that's not their style—but maybe it should be. A good boxing match to leave tangible, unforgivable wounds. Perhaps that's what she's trying to accomplish now.

She's still stabbing herself, blood dripping onto the floor.

"Stop it," Edgar says, reaching out to her. But she can't hear him, and his hand only passes through her shoulder, a chill spreading through his non-being.

Edgar tells himself, maybe there's a way I can move her. He walks into the kitchen, grabs a pad of paper and a pen from the Formica countertop. The clock on the microwave is flashing *POPCORN*.

What the fuck do these people have against time?

Back in the living room, he thinks about opening her Bible so he can scrawl on the pages, but he doesn't know enough about Scripture to make the gesture relevant, and he doesn't want to turn Carolyn into a fire-and-brimstone lunatic.

He writes, GET OUT, then slams the notepad on top of her crimson King James.

She jumps from Ralph's chair, gasping as she looks at the message. A few frantic glances around the room, then she says, "Who's there?"

Now she can see the pen Edgar's holding, no doubt floating from her perspective. He writes, RALPH DOESN'T LOVE YOU!

"Yes he does," she shouts.

Backing away from Edgar—or, more accurately, the floating pen—she loses her footing and falls into the couch. Looking in his direction, but not meeting Edgar's eyes, she says, "What are you? The Devil? Have you come to take me away from my Ralph?"

Edgar damns himself for breaking his code. These people, impossible to help, are a nightmare. The code makes sense, keeps him a voyeur rather than a participant. Now, he senses, the game is changing. And he's in too deep not to make one last effort.

He writes: *Ralph keeps his money in a coffee can on the top shelf of his closet, next to his gun. Take the money and leave. Please start over.* Then, out of desperation—and perhaps a little wickedness—he adds the inscription: *Love, God.* So much for his moral stand. No. She was a nut already.

She closes her eyes, pleads, "Stop it, I don't want to see any more! Please, stop it!"

Edgar picks up the notepad, carries it toward her, then thrusts it in her face. Alarmed by a breeze from his swift action, she opens her eyes and reads the message. Then, slowly, she rises from the couch. Now she's meeting his stare.

Can she see me?

Edgar turns to a mirror, afraid and alternately hopeful that he's somehow become real. But the reflection dashes this notion. The only body in the living room is hers, and she's nodding, a look of understanding taking shape. Without a word, she moves in the direction of the bedroom. And Edgar feels a modicum of relief.

She doesn't deserve to be in this place, and maybe he is here to help her. Relief becomes hope:

If this is my purpose, perhaps tonight will be my last at Sunfall Manor.

She opens the closet and reaches up to Ralph's top shelf, where he keeps his stash of porn in addition to his money and gun. But her hands don't come down with the cash-filled coffee can or the latest issue of *Hustler*.

They come down with the Smith & Wesson, wrapped in a dirty, once-white cloth.

She smiles and says, "I hope your judgment will be merciful, oh Lord." Then she—faster than Edgar can process—puts the barrel of the gun in her mouth and squeezes the trigger.

A blast rings out, smoke billowing from her gaping maw, her brains splattered all over her husband's closet. Carolyn crumples to the shag carpet. The gun clatters against one of the metal support posts of her and Ralph's bed. Her face is pale. Her chest heaves one last time. A blood bubble forms on her lips then pops.

The furnace grinds.

Edgar almost expects to be joined by Carolyn's ghost. *What now, God?* she might say. To which he'll shrug and reply: *Now we make the rounds.* But that doesn't happen. She's gone from this world and his. And he's already tired of playing God.

Edgar sits on the couch and waits. Certainly someone heard the gunshot and called the cops.

Time glides by, but no one comes. He thinks about picking up the phone and dialing 911. But the authorities may not even respond in this ass-crack town without a voice on the other end of the line. Besides, Ralph deserves to find her like this. He needs to understand what *he* did to her.

Or did I, by shining her on, do this?

No. Wherever she is, it's a better place than here. Unless... *What if she's here and I can't see her? Is this place like that goddamn Eagles song?*

"You can checkout any time you like, but you can never leave."

Now he can't get that infernal tune out of his head. And still no one's coming to check on Carolyn. Time feels like hours past *POPCORN.*

Edgar can understand Mike Collins's inaction—the old man's hard of hearing, crazier than a shithouse rat, and doesn't have a phone. But the girl next door and Mac and Art have no excuse. Well, they have excuses aplenty, but none that come close to valid.

Edgar can faintly hear Mac's music upstairs. Mac doesn't know Ralph is away or he'd be blasting Bob Marley or Pink Floyd or rap of some kind. Carolyn never has the nerve to bang on the ceiling or complain, but Ralph threatens Mac with violence as a matter of routine. Much as Edgar hates Ralph, violence against Mac is entirely justified. The guy just needs a beating.

But Mac will have to wait. It's time to visit the girl with many names.

For Edgar, walking through walls feels like passing through a waterfall. A cleansing experience. But his hands are dirty now, and he doesn't think he'll ever be clean again.

The Girl with Many Names

Above her futon is a colorful poster of New York City. Above her toilet, it's Los Angeles. Through her large floor-to-ceiling windows, in a room that's noticeably not of a piece with the house's original construction, a moonlit cornfield sways. The girl's space looks like it's meant for plants, hooks all over the vaulted ceiling. But she had no plants—they would only wilt in her presence—and she never grows.

She's dark. Not just her makeup, always on even though she never leaves, at least not at night, which seems like it would be her time. Why she lives in a converted sunroom is beyond Edgar. She's beyond Edgar. And far more ghostly.

She's in a fetal position in front of the television, watching a show that chronicles a group of struggling models. She likes—or at least watches—reality programs, particularly those that focus on models or actresses or rich socialites. Although the room isn't cold, she's swaddled in winter clothes and thick blankets. She shakes like a junkie, but she doesn't do drugs, at least not the kind that one smokes or snorts or shoots up.

Her drug is the world online. When she's not in front of the television, usually in the small hours of morning, she, the only resident of Sunfall Manor with an Internet connection, is on a website called FriendSpace. She has twenty or more accounts, each with a different profile picture (none of them her) and a different name. Edgar's not even sure what her real name is. The mail strewn across the kitchen table is addressed to many: Beth Johnson, Lyle Anderson, Kayla Sterling... On her nightstand, next to the futon, are three driver's licenses from different states, none of them Nebraska, each reflecting a unique identity.

Edgar first thought the girl was running from something, but she makes her face seen too much for that to be the case. Once a week, three gray-haired men come over. They bring cameras and groceries and money. She fucks them for hours, and they take turns capturing it all on video, available to monthly subscribers on a website called Old Dicks in Young Chicks.

There are no shades or draperies in front of her windows. Anyone walking past can see her in action, but no one ever does. The men sometimes question her lack of discretion, but she just waves off the concern.

She never talks to the men or on camera. In

fact, Edgar's never heard her speak. She just does her business, which she doesn't appear to enjoy or detest, takes their money, and gives them a grocery list of things she needs next week.

Maybe she can't speak. But Edgar doesn't buy that. He suspects that she chooses not to.

The show ends and she turns off the TV. Edgar follows her to the computer, the FriendSpace page already up. She has more than a hundred new notifications from people all over the country.

Get well soon. =)

Sorry to hear about your daughter. My thoughts and prayers are with you.

Hugs Keep your faith in God. It'll get better.

The messages go on and on like that. And she takes her time replying to each of them.

Thank you so much. Knowing I have friends like you makes everything much better. xoxo – Beth.

I never thought something like this could happen to one of my children. Cancer's a terrible disease, but we're blessed with the best doctors, and faith. All the best, Chuck.

Pray for me. My faith is wavering. Does that make me a bad person? Confused in Concord, Mandy.

She never asks her "friends" for money, never seems to take pleasure or pain from the interactions. Typing, fast and accurate, she looks like a machine. A machine working for hours toward no apparent goal. Art would enjoy a TV show about her.

Clack-clack-clack…

She pulls the afghan blanket from her shoulders; puts it over her head and the computer monitor, making a little tent to work in.

Clack-clack-clack…

Bored with watching her, unable to see her anyway, Edgar sits on the futon.

Clack-clack-clack…

She's an exceedingly beautiful girl.

Clack-clack-clack…

A complete mystery.

Clack-clack-clack…

Not unlike a vampire.

Clack-clack-clack…

Draining people of their time and emotions rather than their blood.

Clack-clack-clack…

But to what end?

She gets up, drops the afghan around her shoulders, and walks into the bathroom. Edgar, still thinking that tonight might be his last at Sunfall Manor—hoping it will—gets up from the futon and walks to the computer. He deletes the current message she's working on, replaces it with: *Why do you do this?*

His curiosity is too great to ignore any longer, and he hopes she won't ignore the question.

A piece of black electrical tape covers the lower corner of the screen. Edgar peels it away, and the screen informs him that it's 2:26 p.m. on 3/21/1601. He puts the tape back in place and shakes his head, smiling despite how humorless the whole situation is.

The girl returns and sits down. Looking at the message, she gasps, then glances around the apartment, tears welling in her eyes.

Hands shaking, she clears Edgar's question, then types: *I'm trying to feel.* Then she stares at the screen, obviously waiting for a response, her hands still shaking. She types: *I'm afraid.* Glances around again, then adds: *Thank you.*

A scratching sound comes from one of the large windows, and Edgar and the girl both turn to see a pitiful-looking mutt, one of Art's many Sheppys, flakes of pizza crust in his or her beard.

Dogs scratch at the glass frequently, drawn by the light and a need for companionship. The girl normally ignores them, but now she's reacting differently. She walks to the door, opens it, and waves the dog in. The mutt enters pensively, looking around her place, curiously sniffing the air. She crouches and says, "Did you send me that message?"

So she can speak, though her voice is strange. Nasally. Strained.

Wagging its tail, the dog barks.

"I thought so," she says. "You're more than a dog, aren't you?"

The dog barks again.

"Dog spelled backwards is God. That's who you are."

The dog tilts its head in an inquisitive manner, then puts its paws on her chest, panting.

She puts her arms around it, an ill-at-ease embrace, and says, "You shouldn't have made me this way." The dog licks her face as she runs her hand through the fur of its head and neck. She grabs its head. The dog struggles. She twists hard.

A dull snap. The dog lets out a horrific squeal, then falls to the floor, body twitching.

She stands, looks down at her work, face emotionless. "You shouldn't have made me this way," she repeats. "You did this to yourself." Then she picks up the twitching dog, throws it outside, slams the door.

God is dead, in her mind, although she doesn't appear bolstered by that knowledge.

At the sink of her kitchenette, she washes her hands and face. Grabs a Coke from the refrigerator. Returns to her computer and lights a cigarette.

Clack-clack-clack…

Edgar, shocked and horrified, returns to the futon.

Clack-clack-clack…

And bides his time before he can leave this terrible girl's domain.

– V –

Mac

Edgar can't float—another curveball that initially unbalanced his stance. So he enters the common hallway through the Simmons place (still no response to Carolyn's demise), then moves up the stairs to his next stop.

On his way to Mac's, he tries to forget what happened in the crazy girl's apartment. As horrifying as Carolyn's suicide, the crazy girl tops it. Murder, he reasons, is always more gruesome than suicide. Even if this isn't his last night here, he'll never return to the place of the girl with many names. He'll have to make the cellar his den of solitude, become a spirit world cliché. Of course, he'll have to find a way down there first. The cellar door of the old farmhouse is located outside, so Edgar has never visited the world beneath Sunfall Manor. Sometimes strange noises come from below, piquing his curiosity, but most of those sounds rumble from the furnace. He doesn't know if anyone goes down to the cellar anymore—certainly not repairmen—and wonders if there are more like him trapped down there. No rattling of chains or eerie moans, but he wonders just the same.

He glides through Mac's door.

Mac's real name is Bobby McDonald. Somewhere in his mid-thirties, Mac appears much older, gray creeping into the thin halo of hair around the freckled dome that protects his misfiring brain.

It's always 4:20 at Mac's place, a thing which all the clocks are set to signify. The air is thick with the sweet stench of cannabis, the living room awash in black lights

Mac is entertaining tonight. A skinny blonde, no more than fifteen, is curled up on the couch, snoring. A redhead, no older than the other girl, is nursing a pipe, smoke serpents rising from her lips, which are caked with sparkly lipstick and cold sores. Mac is ass-down in a red beanbag chair, staring up at the dingy ceiling tiles, a stupid grin cracking his face.

Edgar doesn't recognize the song that's thumping from the stereo, assumes it's something one of the girls provided. He hopes that's all they're providing tonight, though he knows better. He's been here too many times not to realize the score. Nowhere else to sit, he cops a squat on the filthy hardwood floor, glad that he's impervious to germs. Well, at least he assumes, having never coughed or sneezed, he is.

The redhead pulls the pipe away from her face, coughs a few times, then turns to Mac. "You sure that wasn't a gun we heard?"

"Look outside," Mac says with blissful indifference. "You see any police cherries out there?"

"No, I just—"

"Shiiiiit," Mac interrupts, "This place is more country than Travis Tritt, Tina. Guns always be going off 'round here. You think you're in Omaha or Lincoln?"

"I'm not Tina," she says, then points at her sleeping friend. "That's Tina."

Mac waves off the correction, slides a hand down his sweatpants, scratches his nuts. And Not-Tina goes back to her pipe. A few shallow tokes, then she says, "Maybe we should call 'em."

Mac bolts upright, anger radiating from his narrowed eyes. Leaning over her, he shouts, "Call who, Tina?"

"I don't know," she drones. And her presence here is all the proof needed to know these are the truest words she'll likely ever speak.

Mac slaps the pipe out of her hand, sending it across the room. Reflexively, reason numbed by bearing witness to such ignorance, Edgar catches the serpent-shaped object. Not-Tina's eyes go wide as she stares at the floating pipe.

"You call the pigs and I'll cut you," Mac threatens.

Not-Tina just keeps staring, her eyes not leaving the pipe until Edgar, realizing his error, drops it. He'd almost been riding the numb zone. This is the place where that happens most frequently. He doesn't think he's capable of a contact high, but he isn't so sure. The haze of this place alone is enough to put anyone or anything into a trance.

"Did you see that?" Not-Tina asks, pointing in the direction of Edgar.

Mac looks stupidly around the room, then turns his less-than-amused attention back on the girl. "See *what?*"

She shakes her head. "You sure you didn't lace that shit with nothing?"

"Did you hear what I said?" Mac snarls.

"W-what?"

"I told you that if you call the cops—"

"Who said anything 'bout calling the cops?"

Dropping back onto his ass, Mac seems content with her answer. He fishes a joint from his shirt pocket, lights it, takes a deep drag. "Don't have to lace my grow," he wheezes. "Shit's the best in the whole damn state."

Not-Tina isn't listening. She falls back in her chair and closes her eyes. Mac returns to studying the ceiling, grin in full glory. Fills his lungs a few more times with smoke, exhales slowly, then puts the joint out in a can of Pabst Blue Ribbon. He shifts his focus between the sleeping girls, grunts derisively a few times, then pulls a wad of cash from his sweatpants—tens and twenties, as far as Edgar can tell—and starts counting. Mac always counts his money when he's alone. Calls it his "cheese." Mac and cheese. *Lovely.* He clearly takes pride in his enterprise, which, Edgar grimly considers, represents the only act of fruit-bearing ambition at Sunfall Manor.

Edgar has nothing against what Mac does for a living. His opinion of *Mac* is another matter. Mac tucks the wad of cash back in his sweats and leans close to Not-Tina. "Hey, baby," he whispers, "wanna have a little fun?"

She stirs. "Huh-uh." Then she puts her hands beneath her head and shifts position, looking like the only thing she's up for is ten to twelve hours of sleep.

Edgar stands, turning away from the matters at hand. He routinely turns his back on Mac's transgressions. But now, listening to Mac undo the girl's belt, thinking about Carolyn, cold and dead downstairs, and the poor dog outside, Edgar can't contain the need for action. He's already laid waste to his code. Why not do it again? He snatches a Zippo and a Burger King bag from the coffee table, sparks the lighter and sets the bag on fire. Then he waves the burning garbage in Mac's face.

"Jesus Christ," Mac shouts, pulling his hand from the girl's jeans and backing away. "What the fuck?"

Not-Tina opens her eyes, sees what Mac sees, and what he's done to her pants, then jumps from the chair. "Dude," she says, buttoning her pants, "this place is haunted." She rushes over to Tina, shakes her. "Hey, bitch," she shouts. "Wake the fuck up!"

Edgar drops the burnt bag, and Mac starts stomping on it, making sure it's out. He says, "This place ain't haunted, girl. Must have just been a breeze or something. This old place is drafty as fuck."

"Breezes don't start shit on fire," Not-Tina says. "Besides, that thing wasn't carried on no breeze. This place is haunted. And you're pretty damn creepy yourself."

Mac heaves a sigh as the real Tina rubs her eyes. "What's happening?" she asks. "I was sleeping."

"We're getting out of here," Not-Tina says. "Your Uncle Bobby's place is haunted."

"Thought I told you to call me Mac," he says in the voice of a hurt child.

"Sorry, Uncle Bobby," Tina says, grabbing her things from the floor and rising on wobbly legs. Then she snaps open her purse, pulls a few crumpled bills from it—twenties—and hands them over to him. "That should cover the smoke."

"Get the fuck out of here," Mac says, grabbing the money.

Flipping him the bird, the girls quickly exit. Mac adds the new bills to his cash. For a moment, he looks like he might count his loot again, but he doesn't. He just shakes his head and slides the wad back into the crotch of his pants. "Didn't want no pussy anyway," he moans.

Edgar feels no sense of righteousness as he watches Mac curl up on the couch and close his eyes. "Didn't want no pussy," Mac repeats, like a punished child going to bed without dessert or a few minutes of *The Tonight Show*.

Edgar sits in the chair that had been occupied by Not-Tina, and Mac starts snoring. Struck by how much he's been alone tonight, Edgar questions why he hasn't put the time to better use. His internal clock tells him it's not 4:20, nor is it *POPCORN* or flashing 12:00. He knows, more importantly, it's not time to leave yet. So he walks to Mac's meager bookshelf, grabs a tattered paperback of *Ubik* by Philip K. Dick—at least Mac pretends to read good books—and sits down again.

Seventy pages in, sure he's read this story before in some kind of life, he knows he can finally leave.

Putting the book down, Edgar thinks about reading another fifty pages, but quickly scratches that idea. He has to move on to the attic, one last stop standing in his way.

Before leaving, a metallic glint catches his eye. He looks at the sword mounted on Mac's wall, then down at Mac, then back at the sword. How easy it would be to snatch the sword, cut Mac into little pieces.

Mac and cheese, please!

He searches himself for violence, hopeful he'll find action worthy of his clear motive. But he comes up empty.

"Some ghost I am," Edgar mutters, then he trudges out of Mac's room, crossing the hall to Mike's place.

– VI –

Mike

At least Mike tries to be something better than he is, standing above the kitchen table in his clown regalia, looking down at a cluster of poorly constructed marionettes while he scratches his head.

Edgar sits down on the other side of the room and glances at Mike's antique grandfather clock. The clock's old, but Mike keeps it in perfect running condition. 3:51 a.m. Only a couple hours 'til dawn.

"Hello, Ladies and Gentleworms," Mike squeals in a strained falsetto, taking the puppet strings into his hands. "Allow me to introduce you to Grim and Cy."

As far as Edgar can tell, the only difference between the two puppets is that Cy has one eye and Grim has two. The same old puppets Mike always uses, now with different names. Then Edgar gets the joke—Cy, short for Cyclops—and laughs. But, much as he hates to admit it, he's laughing at Mike, and that makes him feel bad.

Mike continues his routine, making the puppets argue back and forth in no meaningful way.

"You stole the cookies," Cy says.

"No, you stole the cookies," replies Grim.

Similar banter fills the next few minutes, though it feels much longer to Edgar. The puppets begin to tussle, their wooden legs banging the Formica tabletop, a hectoring cacophony. Mike grabs another puppet with his right hand, awkwardly moving Cy's strings to his left, and the two wooden children become intertwined.

The new puppet has three eyes—two in the right place, the third on its forehead—and a long mane of blonde hair.

"Boys," the new puppet shouts.

"It's Mom," the tangled mess responds twice. Edgar can't tell Cy or Grim apart any longer.

"Violence never solves a thing," Mom says. "Now you boys make up and play nice or it's lights out and no boysenberry pie for you."

Mike tries to untangle his puppets so they can carry out the next scene, but only manages to make a greater mess. Frustrated, he drops the glorified wooden blocks to the table and steeples two fingers beneath his chin.

Edgar applauds politely.

"Still needs something," Mike says. "Still…" Then he snaps his fingers and rushes into the bedroom. A few clatters, thuds, and squeaks later, he returns with a guitar. Strumming, though not creating anything approaching a tune, he sings about a faraway planet named Astrolox, a land where everyone, regardless of race or religion, gets along in peace. Although it sounds like Mike is inventing the lyrics as he goes, Edgar has heard this song many times before. It's always the same—every word, every hesitation—and Edgar once again applauds, though more enthusiastically this time.

Edgar doesn't normally enjoy any of Mike's routines, but now, in light of tonight's grim events, he finds himself viewing Mike through a new filter. The guy's efforts are starting to shine.

Mike honks his bright red nose and says, "That's the ticket to stardom. Yessir, yes indeed." Back at the kitchen table, he shakes a cigarette out of a pack labeled Basic and lights it. He takes a drag, followed by a few unhealthy coughs, then honks his nose again and smiles. "Yes indeed," he repeats.

Mike finishes his victory smoke—he only has one when he's marking an accomplishment. Then Edgar follows him to the bathroom. Mike takes off the clown getup, letting the large yellow suit fall to the floor. He leans over the sink in his underwear and starts to clean the makeup from his face. His dark skin is deeply scarred by burns and blades and other things Edgar can't begin to identify. This is a revelation to Edgar, though hardly shocking.

It doesn't take long for the hot water to fog the mirror, but Mike keeps scrubbing his face without wiping the glass, repeating his mantra: "Yes indeed."

Unable to resist, Edgar writes a message on the misty glass.

YOU'RE GREAT!

Mike opens his eyes and looks at the offering. He studies it for a moment, then smiles. "I always knew I wasn't alone. But…but I can't read, so I don't know what you's tryin' to tell me. Is it good? Do you like my act?"

Edgar nods.

"Been hearin' that *America's Got Talent* is gonna do tryouts in Omaha soon. Tryin' to get my act together to win the million bucks. Think I can do it?"

Edgar draws a crude thumbs-up below his previous message, and Mike's mostly toothless smile becomes a crooked grin, milky makeup running down his dark face. "Really? You really do? I'm what this country needs, you know, good ol' fashion family entertainment. The kind Walt gave us when we was kids." Mike begins singing a mangled version of "When You Wish upon a Star," and Edgar removes himself from the bathroom.

His new friend still singing, Edgar studies the various artifacts on myriad shelves—porcelain clowns and barnyard animals, crystalline angels and rosy-hued cherubs, and photographs, all framed in Wal-Mart's best. A younger version of Mike, looking crazy as ever, stares back at Edgar from a color-faded image, his arm around a younger boy.

Mike steps into the living room, wiping his face with a towel. "You still here?" he says. "Didn't scare you off none with my singin', did I?"

Edgar picks up the photograph and hands it to Mike.

"Good, good. Thought you'd run off on me." He looks at the image. "Ah, you's interested in history. Makes sense, I s'pose. This here is me and my brother, Ty. He went off and died in Vietnam. Me, I couldn't go on account of bein'…well, I couldn't go.

Hey, you're not Ty, are ya? Come back to check in on me?"

Edgar shakes his head. Though he doesn't know who he is, he's sure he isn't Ty Collins. For one, he doesn't feel a particular connection to the sixties. And he's pretty sure he's white, a thought that makes him chuckle. "Of course I'm white," Edgar says. "I'm a ghost."

"If you's Ty, knock somethin' down right now. But don't break anything nice, 'less you is one of them poltergeists or somethin'."

A few silent moments pass, then Mike says, "Nah, didn't think you was Ty. Different handwriting on the mirror. Ty could read and write real good, but even smart folks had a hard time figurin' out his chicken-scratch hand. And I didn't figure you was angry neither. Don't guess angry spirits draw thumbs-ups on crazy folk's mirrors."

Mike sits down on the couch. "Stay for a while if you can, 'less you got some folks to haunt. I don't get many visitors, and I could sure use someone to talk to."

Edgar sits next to Mike.

"All right," Mike says, "move that remote control if you's still here."

Edgar moves the remote an inch, and Mike laughs. "Boy oh boy, this is cool. 'Bout the coolest things that's happened to me since Shadowall."

"Shadowall?" Edgar asks, intrigued.

"Bet you wanna hear about Shadowall," Mike says. "Everyone likes to hear this one, even if they look at me funny while I'm tellin' it, like I'm lyin'. I'm not, but I do tend to ramble. If I ramble on too much, you go ahead and move that there clicker again. I'll know to stop if it moves.

"It started when I was five years old. I'd just come out of the hospital on account of a ruptured 'pendix. Mom says I just 'bout died of fever. Was in there for more'n a month. Pretty scary business for a little guy.

"Anyway, it was my first night back home from the hospital, and I couldn't sleep to save my skin. Just tossin' and turnin', trying to find a comfortable way to the sandman. And that's when it happened. One of the walls of my room lit up real bright. At first I thought it was on account of a passin' car outside my window. But this was more like the wall was…was making its own light…like the light was coming from inside instead of outside.

"I was only five. Didn't know what to make of the whole thing. Heck, I'd been read my last rights and pretty much written off as a goner. So I just stared at the bright wall, thinkin' that God was maybe gonna take me home after all. Wouldn't have hurt me none. The way I'd seen heaven in pictures, with clouds and pretty music, I figured I might just get a good night's sleep up there." Mike laughs. "I sure needed it, too. Still do, as a matter of fact. But ever since Shadowall, I can't sleep at night no more. That's why I worked graveyard shift so many years, down at Henderson's farm, doin' all manner of things that wound my stomach in knots. But that's not what you wanna hear 'bout.

"Shadowall didn't scare me none, not like Henderson's farm did. No sir, it didn't, but I'm afraid that if I'm asleep I might miss it when it comes back. Ain't never seen nothin' else like it. No sir. I hate to do this to you, but can you move that clicker a little if you really want to hear about Shadowall?"

Edgar moves the remote.

"That's so cool," Mike says. "All right, all right. So the wall's so bright that it's got a rainbow halo around it, the way the moon sometimes gets when the clouds're just right. And I'm squintin' real good, my best Clint Eastwood, waiting for somethin' to happen. Suddenly shadows start dancing up there on the wall, just like there's a projector and someone's putting on a show in front of the bulb. But the only projector in town is down at Holiday Drive-In, and, I swear on all that's holy, I'm the only one in the room. For ten nights in a row the most amazin' shows play out on my wall. Dancing girls, which is okay 'cause they was only shadow, and puppets, and dinosaurs, and...well anything you can imagine! It all went right up there on Shadowall—every little thing my heart desired. After every show I slept like I'd never slept before. The best ten nights of my life.

"Then it all went away.

"Now, I know what you're thinkin'. And you're right—I *am* crazy. Made peace with that a long time back, and it don't hurt me none. But I don't think I was too bad back then. I 'spect that fever tore up my brain a good deal—why I can't read. Yessir, I think someone was looking out for me back then. I don't know if it was a guardian angel, or aliens, or any number of weird things. But *it* or *he* or *she* or *they* wanted me to be okay. Move the clicker a little if you're here to bring back Shadowall."

Mike frowns a little when the remote doesn't move, but his smile returns quickly. "Yeah, was afraid of that. Still, this is pretty cool, talkin' to a ghost and all. Bet you was a nice person who did a bunch of good things for others. Someone real special and important. Whatever you are…thank you."

And with that, Mike closes his eyes and falls asleep, a look of contentment on his face.

– VII –

Cry from Below

Edgar hears the piercing whine the moment he steps into the hallway. Instead of going up to the attic, he moves down the stairs, the teakettle cry growing louder with every step. It dawns on Edgar that Mac isn't asleep because he's too high, and Mike isn't the victim of childlike exhaustion. He's also sure that Art and Carolyn and the girl with many names aren't downstairs having a tea party.

On the first-floor landing, he peeks into Art's apartment. Art is sprawled on the floor.

Edgar looks through the window in the foyer. No sign of Ralph's car yet. Then he looks in on Carolyn. She's still dead. He considers going down to the cellar to locate the ruptured gas line. But how? He can move through walls, not floors and ceilings. Shaking his head, he returns to the second floor landing, thinks about the cellar one last time, and then takes the narrow stairway to the attic.

A little less than an hour before sunrise, this is the most attic time Edgar's ever been granted, and he doesn't want to waste another second.

– VIII –

The Attic

The newspapers are arranged in two different sets. The west side makes up those Edgar has gone through; the east side, those he hasn't. Although he doesn't read every word, Edgar scans the headlines of each story and always pays special attention to the obituaries.

Now he's working though the papers at a fast clip, still being careful not to miss a single page. Mercifully, the papers, though plentiful, aren't dense publications. He breezes past world news stories about Iran Contra and Oliver North, skims local reports about bake sales and corn carnivals and Big Red football, drags his finger down the obits, looking for anything that tracks. Paper after paper, nothing does.

Then...

Allan Dale Poe, 24 years of age, of Sunfall, died Tuesday, September 25, 1989, as a result of an accident in the family home where he was residing. He was born on March 21, 1965, in Lincoln, Neb., to Dale and Jane Poe. He is survived by his mother, Jane.
At the family's request, no services are scheduled.

No longer Edgar, Allan looks up, consumed by a flood of memories and a wave of sorrow. He remembers that Art Stillwater's living room was once his bedroom. The south wall of the attic suddenly becomes bright, just like Mike's childhood memory, a rainbow halo expanding...expanding...

And Allan remembers everything.

Home

1989

A llan couldn't leave. His mother needed him. Ever since his father's death the previous winter, the result of a motorcycle accident, Jane Poe's drinking had become reason for grave concern, forcing Allan to withdraw from grad school at UNL and move home. Although he held onto his job at The Book Rack, a used bookstore in nearby Lincoln, which allowed him to escape three times a week (Monday, Wednesday, and Friday), it wasn't enough. He missed his apartment, his friends, and his classes. He missed his life.

When his mother had started dating a new man, Allan hoped she would be okay, looked after. But Kyle Irvin, ten years younger than her and filled with rage, was in even worse condition than her. Allan did his best to isolate himself in his room at night, where he would try to read. But dire arguments either bled through the walls, or he was afraid they might at any moment. Either way, he was a nervous wreck, unable to enjoy a moment's peace in the family home.

"He's poisonous," he'd told his mother that morning.

"That's not a nice thing to say," she'd said, scrambling him eggs for breakfast. "Besides, not everything's awful. You've got me to do your laundry and cook for you."

"Yeah, Mom, but that's not what I'm talking about. You're fine a lot of the time, but when you start drinking around him, you seem to lose yourself. I don't want to see anything bad happen, and I can tell that Kyle isn't our kind of guy."

"What kind of guy is he then? I like him, makes me feel young. Don't you want your old mom to be happy?" Her bloodshot eyes spoke of anything but happiness.

Of course he wanted her to be happy, but there was no reasoning with her. Still, she was right about one thing, though it was no thanks to her. Not everything was awful.

The previous day at the bookstore, he'd met a girl. She had auburn hair not held aloft by copious Aqua Net—a fad he wished would die soon—sunkissed cheeks, and the deepest, most stunning emerald eyes he'd ever seen. More importantly, she was smart. A third year Creative Writing student, she shared his fondness for speculative fiction.

She was flipping through *Deathbird Stories* by

Harlan Ellison, wearing a Depeche Mode *101* concert tee, when he approached and asked, "Is there anything I can help you find?"

"Yeah, do you have any Philip K. Dick?"

"Get that question all the time," he said. "No. Most everything's out of print, and the second we get something of his, it's gone before we can shelve it. Let me guess, you just saw *Blade Runner* for the first time?"

She laughed and shook her head. "Fair assumption. I'm doing a paper on his Exegesis theories, and the one copy of *Valis* in the school's library seems to have gone missing. The assignment is to write about an author and his or her madness, and I'd sooner chew off my arm than write about L. Ron Hubbard."

"You could always take on Lovecraft."

"Nah, he was just a prick who wrote about madness."

"Blasphemy," he said with mock indignation. They both laughed.

They talked for more than an hour about their favorite authors. Hers were Frederik Pohl and Anne Rice. His were Robert Heinlein and Spider Robinson, which she said meant he was conflicted.

"How so?" he asked.

"One's a fascist, the other's so liberal he's damn near a card-carrying member of the Communist Party."

They playfully argued, and he poked fun at her for reading sexy vampire novels. As they laughed and flirted, he counted three times she played with her hair, something he'd always heard meant a girl was interested. And she batted her eyelashes a lot—

another tell-tale sign. Not that he'd ever paid attention to such things…until now, when it seemed like it finally mattered.

She looked at her watch and said, "I'm going to be late for class if I don't get going."

"What are you doing Friday night?" he asked.

"Nothing that can't be done some other time. Why?"

"Let me take you out to dinner. I get off work at seven. You can meet me here. And if a copy of *Valis* comes through the door in the meantime, I'll be sure to save it for you."

"Seven sounds great," she said with a smile. Then she offered her right hand. "My name's Ann."

"Ah, like Anne Rice," he said, holding her hand but not shaking it.

"No e at the end I'm afraid, and I can't write near as well. Not yet."

"My name's Allan," he said.

"Ann and Allan," she said. "That…has a nice ring to it."

"I think so."

They slowly let go of each other, fingers trailing across palms.

"Friday," she said.

"Friday," he agreed. "Just like the Heinlein novel."

She pretended to gag, then shot him one last smile as she exited the store.

On his way home, he stopped at a little bookstore that he knew in Seward. And, serendipity in full swing, they had a copy of *Valis* and *A Scanner Darkly*. So he picked the books up, and basked in good feelings all the way home.

Allan was pulled from his reverie by an all-too-familiar disharmony, dust-filled rays no longer bleeding through the blinds of his sole window. Good feelings were gone. It was night, the time of discontent, a hectoring song by John Cougar Mellencamp blasting in the living room, but not loud enough to drown the sounds of fresh violence.

Allan bolted from his room.

He gasped when he saw the scene playing out in the living room. His mother's wrists tied behind her back, Kyle repeatedly backhanded her across the face. She cried for him to stop, but his maniacal expression didn't betray human limitations or any level of decency. He didn't even have the tact to take his debauchery into the bedroom.

"Get the fuck out of our house!" Allan shouted, drawing Kyle's attention away from his victim.

"Hey, sport," Kyle said with a grin, "we're just playing a little game is all. Consenting adults and all—you know how it is? So head back to your room and mind your own pecker, okay?"

Tears flooded his mother's face, terror radiating from her eyes. Allan was sure this wasn't a consensual game. Standing his ground, though Kyle was nearly twice his size, Allan shook his head and said, "No! Either you get out of here or I'm calling the cops." Then, looking at his mother, he cringed at the sight of her bloody nose and black eye, trying to determine if she needed immediate medical attention. "You okay, Mom?" he asked dumbly, at a loss for anything better to say.

"Just go into your room, sweetie" she said, breathing heavily. "I'll…I'll be fine."

"Bullshit," Allan said, shifting his attention back

on Kyle, who crossed his arms, looking like some kind of roadhouse bouncer.

"You heard the lady," Kyle said. "Scram!"

"No way, asshole," Allan said, "I need you to get out of here or I'm—"

But he never finished the sentence. Kyle stormed across the room and punched him in the face. The world spun crazily, his mother's crying intensified, then he blacked out.

***

He was brought back to consciousness by the stench of gasoline. His hands were bound behind his back, and he was on his knees with his head pressed against the south wall of his bedroom. Pain screamed through his head, his body numb with shock.

Moonlight cast Kyle's shadow onto the wall, looming large in Allan's cloudy gaze. A fresh splash of gasoline fell into Allan's eyes, and he screamed.

"Told you to mind your own business," Kyle said.

"Don't hurt him," Allan's mother pleaded from the other room.

"You're crazy," Allan said, frantically trying to blink away the burn.

Kyle snapped his Zippo repeatedly, leaning his head over Allan's shoulder.

Click—clack. Click—clack.

"You're gonna do time for this," Allan threatened.

Click—clack. Click—clack.

"Jesus Chris," Allan cried, "just leave us alone."

Click—clack. Click—clack.

"I'm not going to—"

A bright ball of flame filled his vision, cutting off his words, a million jagged needles blazing through his marrow. He screamed…and screamed…until the fire engulfed his throat, pain escalating past reason, suffocating him as he felt his flesh melt and heard his mother weep.

"Damn it, kid!" Kyle shouted. "Was just trying to scare you. Didn't have to get so close to the—"

Then Allan's hearing went with a painful pop and a shrill scream, his body falling into itself, losing sense of gravity, of time, of self.

The last thought he clung to: Ann. Their date on Friday…how sorry he was that he wouldn't make it. Maybe some other time…maybe…

Then nothing.

– X –

Shadowall and the Cellar

An image of what might have been, two shadows grace the brightly lit wall. One of them is clearly a representation of Allan; the other, Ann. Dancing to a song that can't be heard. "Ann and Allan"—she liked the sound of that, and so did he. Elegantly, lovingly, they move.

But the ghost of Allan is frozen, the newspaper, open to his obituary, still lying in his lap.

Finally, although still transfixed by Shadowall, he manages to stand. He traces Ann's outline with a gentle touch. Presses harder. And his hand penetrates the wall, a partition that doesn't lead into another room of the house. Where it goes, he doesn't know. But he wants to find out soon. He extends his hand to another wall, one that leads into the night. His hand goes through. He's no longer a prisoner.

He wants to leave. To run free. For now, however, there's still unfinished business at Sunfall Manor, and the dawn is fast approaching.

He scampers down the narrow stairwell. Dashes into Mac's place and grabs the Zippo and the cell phone from the coffee table.

Click—clack. Click—clack.

Then he rushes into the kitchen, finds what he's looking for—a phonebook— with a stack of dirty dishes on top of it. He snatches the book, dishes tumbling down, shattering on the floor.

Back in Mac's living room, Allan throws the directory open, turns to P, runs his finger down the page until he finds a listing for J. Poe, the only Poe in the book. He punches in her number, presses *send*, and waits.

One ring…two…three…four—

"You've reached the phone of Jane Poe," the older but still recognizable voice says. "If you're interested in an apartment at Sunfall Manor, please leave your name and number after the beep. We're filled to capacity currently, but vacancies can happen at any time, and I'd be more than happy to add your name to the waiting list."

Beep.

Though he knows she can't hear his voice, he says, "Hi, Mom. Remember me? Just read about my 'accident' in the paper. Know I'm a little late to the party, but…I'm coming for you. I can't say for sure how I know it, but I'm coming for you. Soon!" He presses *end* and tosses the phone at Mac, who's still breathing, but in a strained, shallow manner.

Sunfall Manor is ripe and ready to bloom.

In the hallway, ready to rush back to the attic, he's stopped by a loud metallic clanking that's echoing up the stairwell. The teakettle hiss is now gone, and he wonders if someone is fixing the leak. One thing's for sure, someone or some*thing* is banging on the pipes in the cellar. Briskly, he follows the noise downward.

Click—clack. Click—clack.

He's not even aware he's playing with the lighter, his focus intent on the sounds from the cellar, growing louder as he descends.

Clang…clang…clang…

Click—clack. Click—clack.

He walks through the front door, greeted by a gentle breeze. It feels good on his face, doesn't seem to go through him, and he smiles.

Crows caw. Dogs bark. The corn rustles.

The night, so unlike Sunfall Manor, is alive. The low moon is curved like a question mark in the star-sprinkled sky.

Click—clack. Click—clack.

Clang…clang…clang…

He moves around the house quickly, mindful of the moon's position, aware that time is short, and stops at the cellar door.

Click—clack. Click—clack.

Clang…clang…clang…

He is afraid to go below, senses that something terrifying is waiting for him there. But he also knows he has no choice.

Click—clack. Click—clack.

Clang…clang…clang…

Through the door, he enters the filthy, cob-webbed space, and the clanging suddenly stops, something moving in the darkness. Guided by the moonlight, bleeding through a broken windowpane, he navigates his way down crumbling stone steps.

With a click, a light bulb comes alive. Holding the light's cord in one hand and a wrench in the other, Kyle Irvin sneers at Allan. "Who the hell are you?" Kyle says.

"You don't recognize me?" Allan asks angrily.

Click—clack. Click—clack.

Kyle jumps back, a shocked look on his face. "You can see me? You can hear me?" Then he looks down at the lighter in Allan's hand and smiles. "And you brought me a little present, too. Just what I was looking for."

Allan, filled with rage, doesn't know what to do. Here he is, faced with his own murderer, but the man—the ghost—evidently doesn't know who he is. Just like Allan, he's a prisoner, looking for a means of escape.

Click—clack. Click—clack.

"Come on, friend," Kyle says with a smile, "Don't just stand there. Bring me that torch and let me send this place to the moon."

Now consciously aware of the Zippo, Allan brings it to his face. Stares at it. And sees a reflection in the lighter's golden sheen, though not of his face. Reflected back, Kyle's yellow-toothed grin on that long-ago night.

"Kyle Irvin," Allan says, then casts his eyes on the other ghost in the cellar.

A dumbfounded look envelops Kyle, and he takes a few steps backward, awareness and recognition dancing in his eyes. "Holy shit," he moans. "Holy fuckin' shit."

Click—clack. Click—clack.

"Look, kid," Kyle says, a nervous smile taking shape, "let's say you light this candle and we'll let God sort everything out."

"I don't believe in God."

"Well, then we'll let the devil take a stab at our grudge."

"Don't believe in him, either."

"C'mon, kid. We both know that what I done was wrong, and that it was an accident, right?"

Allan shakes his head.

"Man, I've been trapped down here in the dark for longer than I know. Turn the light on only when I need to, when I get scared down here, so it don't burn out on me. I…I think I've paid plenty for my sins."

"I know why I'm here," Allan says, "but why are you?"

"Your mom felt sorry for me, let me move in after you died. I had nowhere else to go after spending the last of my money on the trial."

"The trial?"

"Yeah, your mom and me cooked up a little suicide note for you, but certain authorities weren't buying it."

"And…"

"Well, I got off. Not enough evidence to convict me. But your mom, best woman I ever knew, took me in, let me stay down here in the cellar. Set up a bed for me and everything. Never let me have my way with her again, but I didn't mind none. Whatever you do, don't be mad at your mama. She was a real God-fearing woman. Got her life together, too.

"But I couldn't. I was really sorry for what I done to you, still am, and I drank myself to death down here. I don't know no more than that, and I didn't even know all that 'fore you came down here."

"That's all I needed to know," Allan says, then he moves toward the exit.

"Where you going?" Kyle says.

But Allan doesn't reply, just turns and watches Kyle's furious advance.

Kyle swings a clenched fist. But it only goes through Allan, throwing Kyle off balance. He stumbles across the cracked floor, then looks up angrily and says, "Give me that fuckin' lighter."

Allan moves toward the cellar door, shaking his head. In a flash, Allan's outside again, Kyle pounding on the other side of the door. "Get back here," he says. "Get back here and set me free."

Click—clack. Click—clack.

***

In the attic, the two dancing forms are still graceful on the south wall as Allan enters and hears a car pull up to the house. He looks out a thin rectangular window and sees Ralph's car, dimly visible in the purple, pre-dawn haze. Ralph slams the car door and ambles toward the house.

Ann and Shadow-Allan break into swing moves as Allan breaks newspapers into smaller stacks, spreading them evenly across the floor.

The Simmons' door slams downstairs as Allan finishes his work. He waits, then enjoys the sound of Ralph's scream. "Serves the fucker right," he whispers.

Click—clack. Click—clack.

Allan's only concern is for Mike. But Mike's old, doesn't have much time left. And he wouldn't have minded God taking him home when he'd been only five. *Yes indeed*, Mike will be just fine, performing his puppet shows for angels like himself. This cruel world isn't good enough for guys like Mike.

Allan flicks the lighter, which ignites a pocket of gas in the air. He jerks back with a laugh. *This is going to be fun*, he thinks.

Ann and Shadow-Allan are really swinging now.

Click—clack. Click—clack.

He doesn't care what happens to Kyle Irvin. Kyle's already dead, and there's nothing he can do about him. He knows what he needs to know— what the newspaper already alluded to—that his mother was complicit in his death. Vengeance will be his. He doesn't know how, but he knows his target. And the way things are playing out, he's sure she's just beyond Shadowall. Maybe even waiting for him. The clockwork of death, far more precise than that of the living, is his.

Moving across the floor quickly, he applies the Zippo's flame to the stacks of newspapers, then stands back, watching the floor disappear beneath a bluish wall of fast-moving madness.

Flames crackle.

An explosion bellows.

Glass shatters.

Shadow-Allan picks up Ann and spins her around his back, her skirt flying high.

Click—clack. Click—clack.

Allan drops the lighter to the floor, then,

through the raging fire, grins as he runs at Shadowall.

He leaps—

Shadowall darkens.

—and crashes against the exposed studs of the now-naked wall, a cold barricade once more. Pain slicing through his side, Allan falls to the burning floor with a whimper.

Another explosion sounds. Allan's world tilts sideways.

Then he's falling…

…pain beyond reason screaming through his burning body…

No, his mind screams. *No! This isn't fair!* Then again, life was never fair. Why should death be any different?

Wrapped in darkness, wishing that awareness and pain would die, though they don't, he keeps burning and falling…

Click—clack. Click—clack.

…burning and falling…

Click—clack. Click—clack.

…burning and falling through a timeless void…

…burning and falling for eternity.

THE END

ABOUT THE AUTHOR

Peter Giglio (an active member of the HWA) is a Pushcart nominated novelist, editor, and screenwriter. His novels include *Anon, Beyond Anon,* and *The Dark* (with Scott Bradley). *Sunfall Manor* is his third published novella and the first in a series of long works set in the small fictional town of Sunfall, Nebraska. Peter's work has been published or is forthcoming from Black Dog & Leventhal (New York), Etopia Press, Dark Moon Books, Ravenous Shadows, and Nightscape Press, to name a few. He's actively (with co-writer Scott Bradley) shopping a feature-length screen adaptation of Joe R. Lansdale's *"The Night They Missed the Horror Show,"* with a strong endorsement from Mr. Lansdale, and is working on (under option) a screen adaptation of Rick Hautala's *Little Brothers*. In addition, the film rights for *Sunfall Manor* are currently under option by an established screenwriting team based in Los Angeles. Peter always has time for readers at <u>petergiglio.com</u>, Facebook, and <u>petergiglioauthor.blogspot.com</u>